D00046434

I wish I could...

Swim with the SHARKS

Written by Gordy Slack
Illustrated by Nancy King

Dr. Douglas Long, scientific advisor

CALIFORNIA ACADEMY OF SCIENCES

in cooperation with Roberts Rinehart Publishers

Acknowledgments
Thanks to Jerry Kay, Linda Allison and William S. Wells,
whose 1987 book, *Sharks*, in the Academy's Science In Action Learning Series,
served as the springboard for this book.

Cover and book design by Archetype, Inc., Denver, Colorado

International Standard Book Number 1-57098-116-7
Library of Congress Catalog Card Number 96-72305

Published by Roberts Rinehart Publishers
5455 Spine Road
Boulder, Colorado 80301
303.530.4400

In cooperation with the California Academy of Sciences
Golden Gate Park
San Francisco, California 94118

Published in the UK and Ireland by
Roberts Rinehart Publishers
Trinity House, Charleston Road
Dublin 6, Ireland

Distributed to the trade by Publishers Group West

Manufactured in Hong Kong

I wish I could...

Swim with the SHARKS

I wish I could swim
with the sharks.

FISH

Welcome to
my world.
Whoa! How'd we get here?
Yikes! Are you sure
this is safe?
I don't know, but
it sure is cool.

Let me explain something about what makes a shark a shark.

- Sharks are fishes that have no bones. Instead, their skeletons are made out of cartilage, the same substance that is at the tip of your nose. But shark cartilage is harder than human cartilage.
- Shark skin is very tough. It is covered with tiny, hard, tooth-like scales called denticles. Some shark skin is so abrasive that if one of these sharks rubs against you, it would badly scratch your skin.
- Sharks have from five to seven gill openings on each side of their head. Bony fishes have only one.
- Unlike other fishes, sharks don't have gas bladders to help them stay afloat. Most sharks need to keep moving forward or they will sink to the bottom.
- Sharks belong to the class of animals called Chondrichthyes (pronounced con·drick·these) that also includes sawfish, skates, and rays.

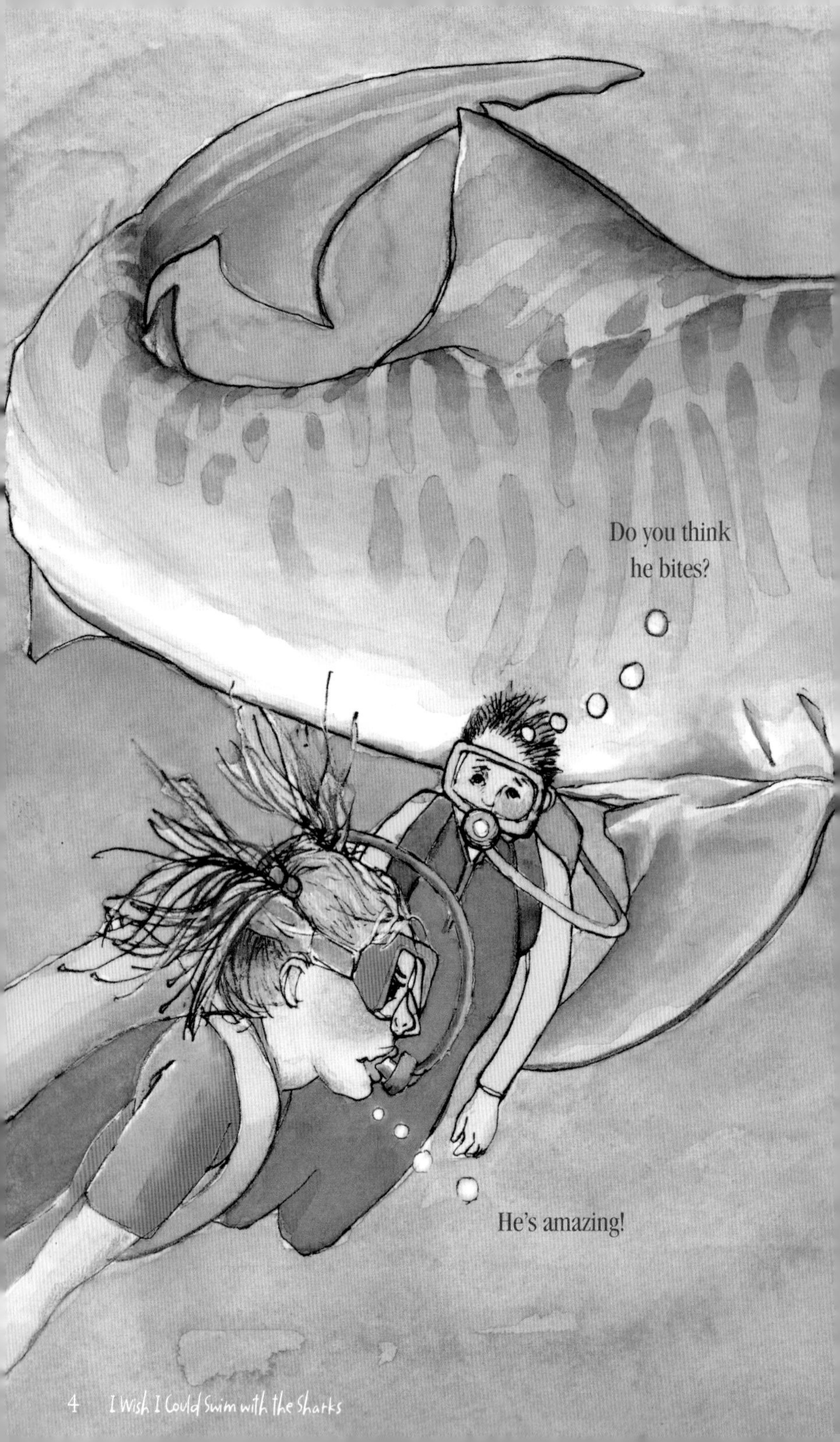
Do you think he bites?
He's amazing!

Many sharks are fast swimmers. Their powerful muscles, streamlined forms, and flexible bodies allow them to swim easily through the water. You usually can recognize a shark by the way it bends its body as it swims.

Organs of Lorenzini

Sharks also have an extra sense. They use small detectors along their snout to sense slight changes in electrical current. These detectors are called organs of Lorenzini and they help sharks to zero in on prey.

Sharks are good at smelling, too. Two-thirds of a shark's brain is devoted to smelling. A shark can smell a few drops of blood in the water up to a quarter mile away.

Some sharks can be ferocious hunters and some even have a reputation for attacking people.

There are more than 350 different kinds, or species, of sharks.

And new species are discovered by scientists every year. They come in all shapes and sizes. Let's meet some of the record holders.

His mouth is even bigger than yours.

Shut up!

The whale shark is not only the biggest shark, it's the biggest fish of any kind. Some whale sharks have been reported at more than 50 feet long—as long as a school bus. And they can weigh as much as 40,000 pounds. Are they dangerous? Not unless you're a small shrimp or a tiny fish. They get all of their food by sifting these small animals out of the water and rarely eat anything larger than a minnow.

Whale Shark
Rhincodon typus
World's Biggest

The smallest shark may be the dwarf dogfish shark. When fully grown, at fewer than eight inches long, one could fit in the palm of your hand.

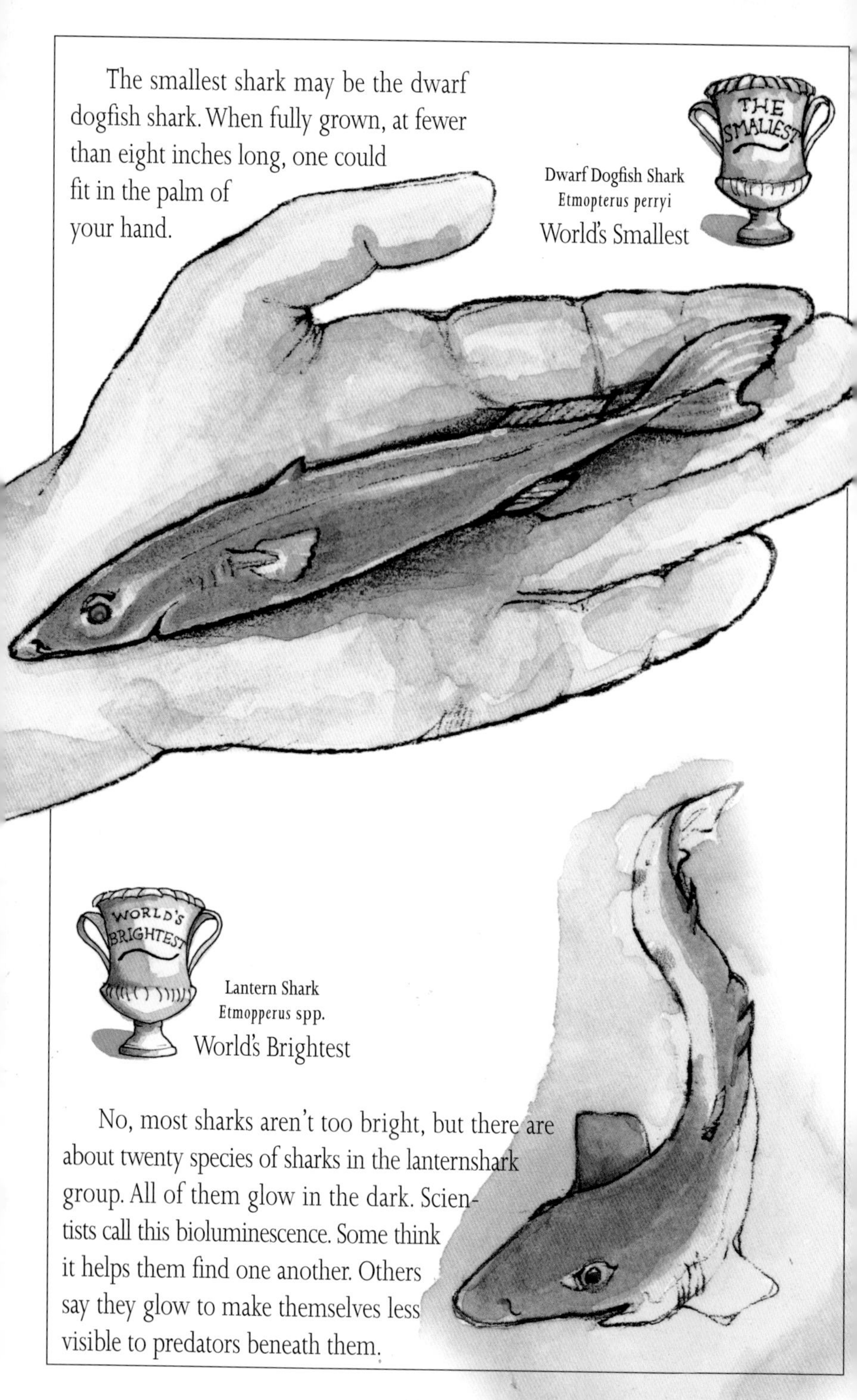

Dwarf Dogfish Shark
Etmopterus perryi
World's Smallest

Lantern Shark
Etmopperus spp.
World's Brightest

No, most sharks aren't too bright, but there are about twenty species of sharks in the lanternshark group. All of them glow in the dark. Scientists call this bioluminescence. Some think it helps them find one another. Others say they glow to make themselves less visible to predators beneath them.

The great white shark is one of the world's largest and most ferocious predators of any kind.

Great White Shark
Carcharodon carcharias
World's Scariest

There are a lot of bizarre sharks, but the weirdest looking is the goblin shark, which lives in very deep water. Its skin is white or pale gray and is almost see-through. Because it lives 1,500 feet below the ocean's surface, the goblin is rarely caught and little is known about its life or its biology.

Goblin Shark
Mitsukurina owstoni
World's Weirdest

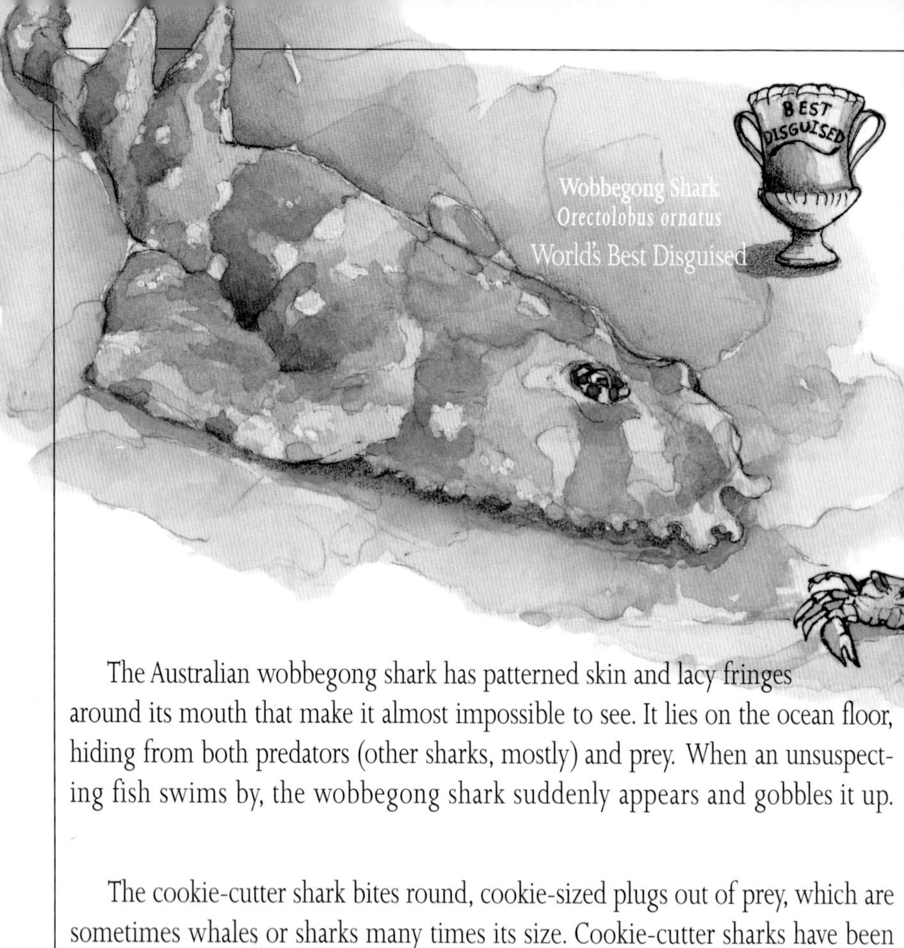

Wobbegong Shark
Orectolobus ornatus
World's Best Disguised

The Australian wobbegong shark has patterned skin and lacy fringes around its mouth that make it almost impossible to see. It lies on the ocean floor, hiding from both predators (other sharks, mostly) and prey. When an unsuspecting fish swims by, the wobbegong shark suddenly appears and gobbles it up.

The cookie-cutter shark bites round, cookie-sized plugs out of prey, which are sometimes whales or sharks many times its size. Cookie-cutter sharks have been known to attack submarines, perhaps mistaking them for whales.

Cookie-Cutter Shark
Isistius brasiliensis
World's Best Cookie Maker

The thresher shark's tail may be as long as the rest of its body. It uses its tail to crowd schooling fish into a small area. It whips the frantic fish with its tail, stunning some and killing others. Then it eats them.

Thresher Shark
Alopias vulpinus
World's Best Tail

The rare frill shark lives in cool, deep water. The frilly collar around its throat is actually the edge of its first gill opening.

Frill Shark
Chlamydoselachus anguineus
World's Fanciest

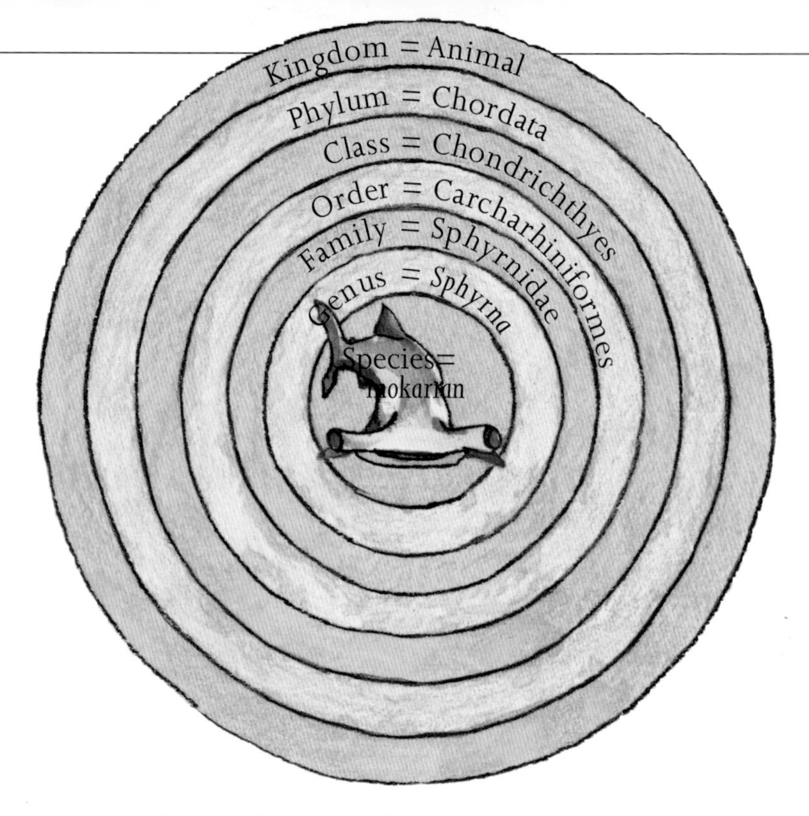

Are all the different kinds of sharks related?

Sure. In my family, for instance, there are eight different species of sharks. But altogether there are 28 different families, including more than 350 different species.

Scientists study and compare different species of sharks to determine how they are related to each other. This kind of science helps to trace the evolutionary history of sharks. The animal kingdom is divided into groups called phyla. These are further divided into classes, orders, families, genera, and species. Sharks are in the phylum Chordata (vertebrates); the class Chondrichthyes (fish with cartilage); and the order Carcharhiniformes (sharks). Each shark has a scientific name made of its genus and its species. The great hammerhead shark, for example, is in the genus *Sphyrna* and the species *mokarran*. So its scientific name is *Sphyrna mokarran*.

It takes a long time for such a wide variety of animals to evolve. All modern sharks share a common ancestor which lived about 400 million years ago. Humans, by comparison, have only been around for about two and a half million years.

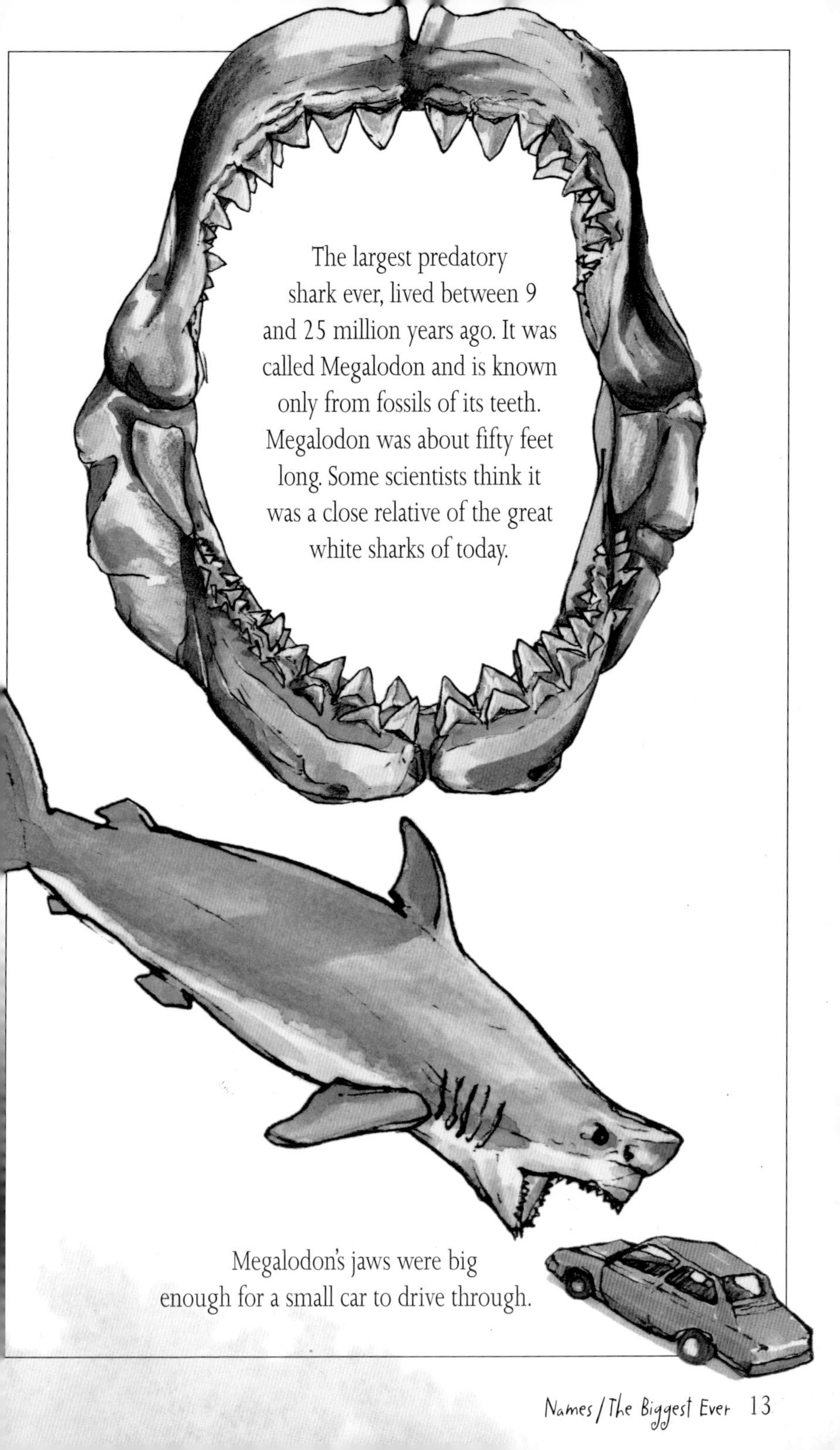

The largest predatory shark ever, lived between 9 and 25 million years ago. It was called Megalodon and is known only from fossils of its teeth. Megalodon was about fifty feet long. Some scientists think it was a close relative of the great white sharks of today.

Megalodon's jaws were big enough for a small car to drive through.

You can tell a lot about an animal by its teeth.

Like how much candy it eats?

Like whether it eats plants or meat, you mean?

Yes. For example, look at the great white shark's teeth, compared to the dogfish shark's.

Dogfish shark teeth: designed for crushing shellfish

Great white shark tooth: designed for tearing flesh

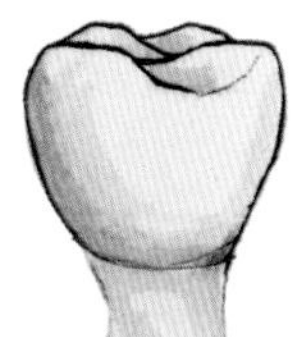

Human tooth: designed for chewing meat and vegetables.

Sharks have special teeth. They are arranged in rows and as the exposed teeth break off or wear down new ones grow to replace them. A great white shark might have hundreds of teeth in its lifetime.

All kinds of things.

So what do sharks eat with all of those teeth?

Some sharks eat shellfish, lobster, crab, fish, seals, dolphins, even other sharks. Sharks don't spend a lot of time chewing. They just tear into their food with razor-sharp teeth, ripping off hunks. Sometimes they just swallow their food whole.

Sharks have roomy jaws. They are made to take huge bites. Some sharks open their mouths wide enough to swallow a whole seal.

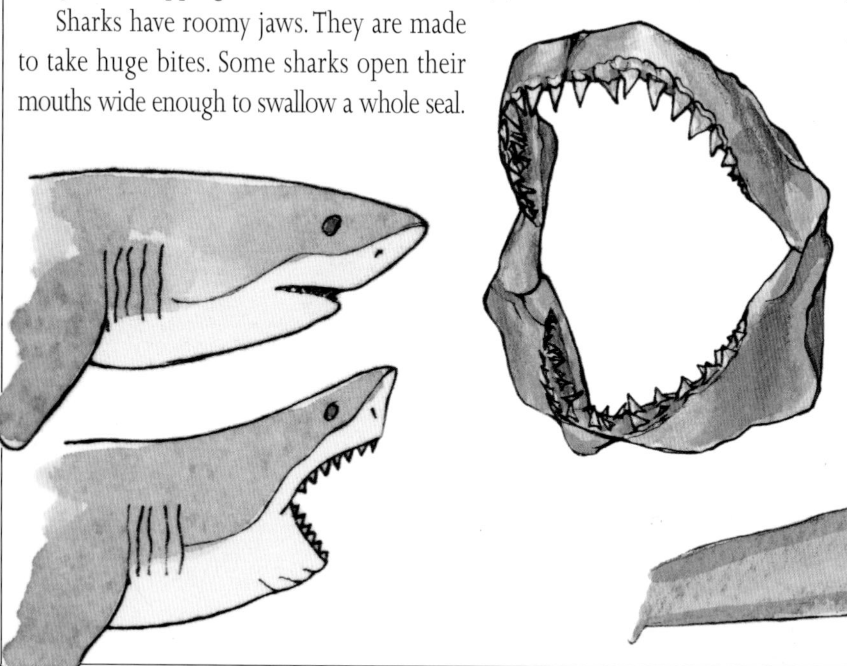

Amazing things have been found in sharks' stomachs. The stomach of a 12-foot gray shark from Australia had eight legs of mutton, half a lamb, and the hind quarters of a pig. Other sharks' stomachs have contained a dog, half a crocodile, tin cans, bicycle parts, and the hind section of a horse.

After a big shark has a good meal, it may go for a month or more before it eats again.

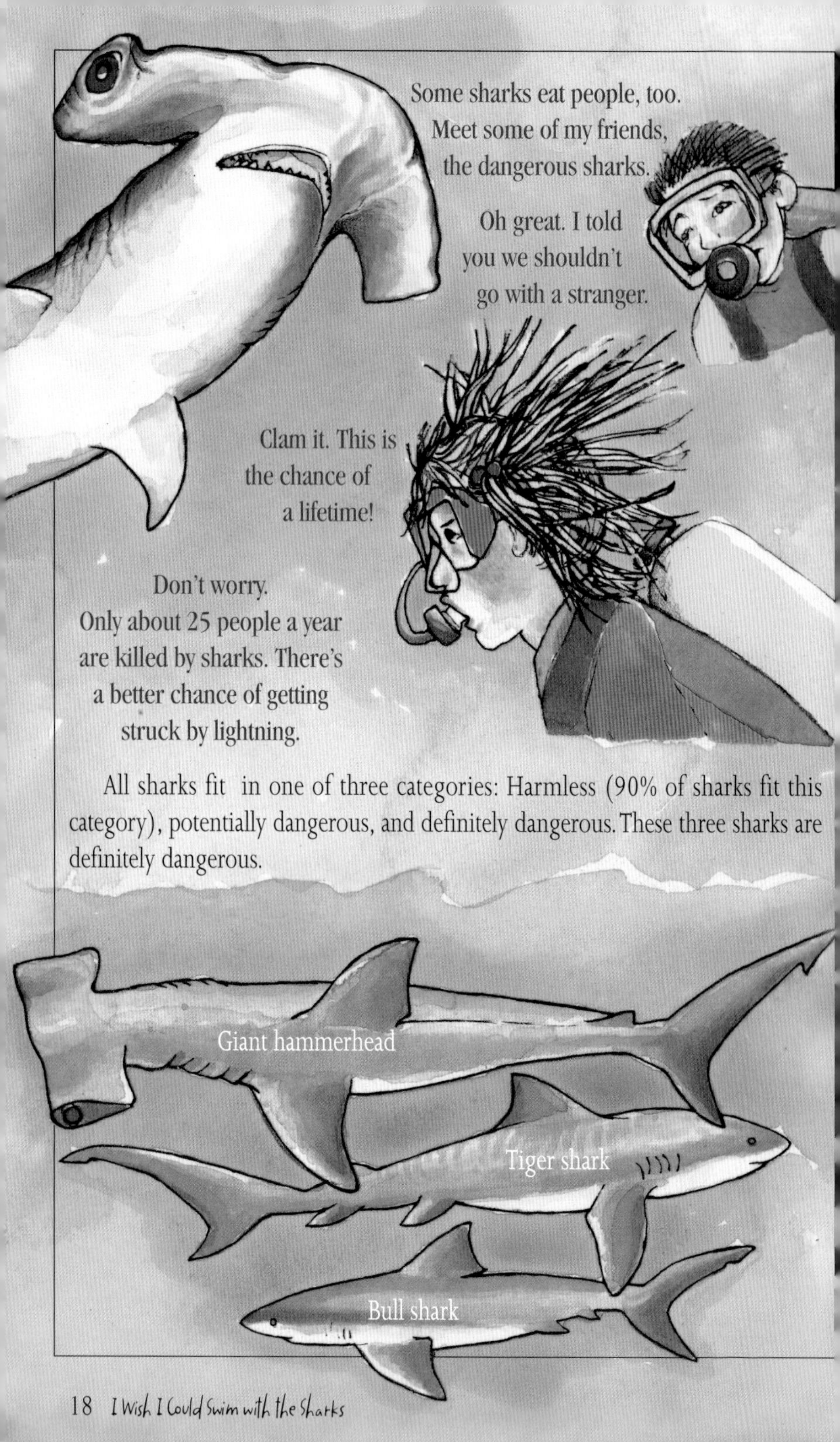

Some sharks eat people, too. Meet some of my friends, the dangerous sharks.

Oh great. I told you we shouldn't go with a stranger.

Clam it. This is the chance of a lifetime!

Don't worry. Only about 25 people a year are killed by sharks. There's a better chance of getting struck by lightning.

All sharks fit in one of three categories: Harmless (90% of sharks fit this category), potentially dangerous, and definitely dangerous. These three sharks are definitely dangerous.

The most famous dangerous shark of all is the great white shark. Great whites live in all the oceans but are most common in the cool coastal waters of North America, southern Africa, and southern and western Australia. Unfortunately, we know little about how many white sharks exist, how often they breed, or whether they migrate. Two things we do know for sure: white sharks are very rare and they sometimes attack people. Humans are not normal prey for great whites and they sometimes spit out their first bite of a person and swim away.

Great whites sometimes attack surfers, probably thinking that they are seals. After one shark attack a scientist studied the bite missing from the surfboard and concluded the shark was at least 18 feet long.

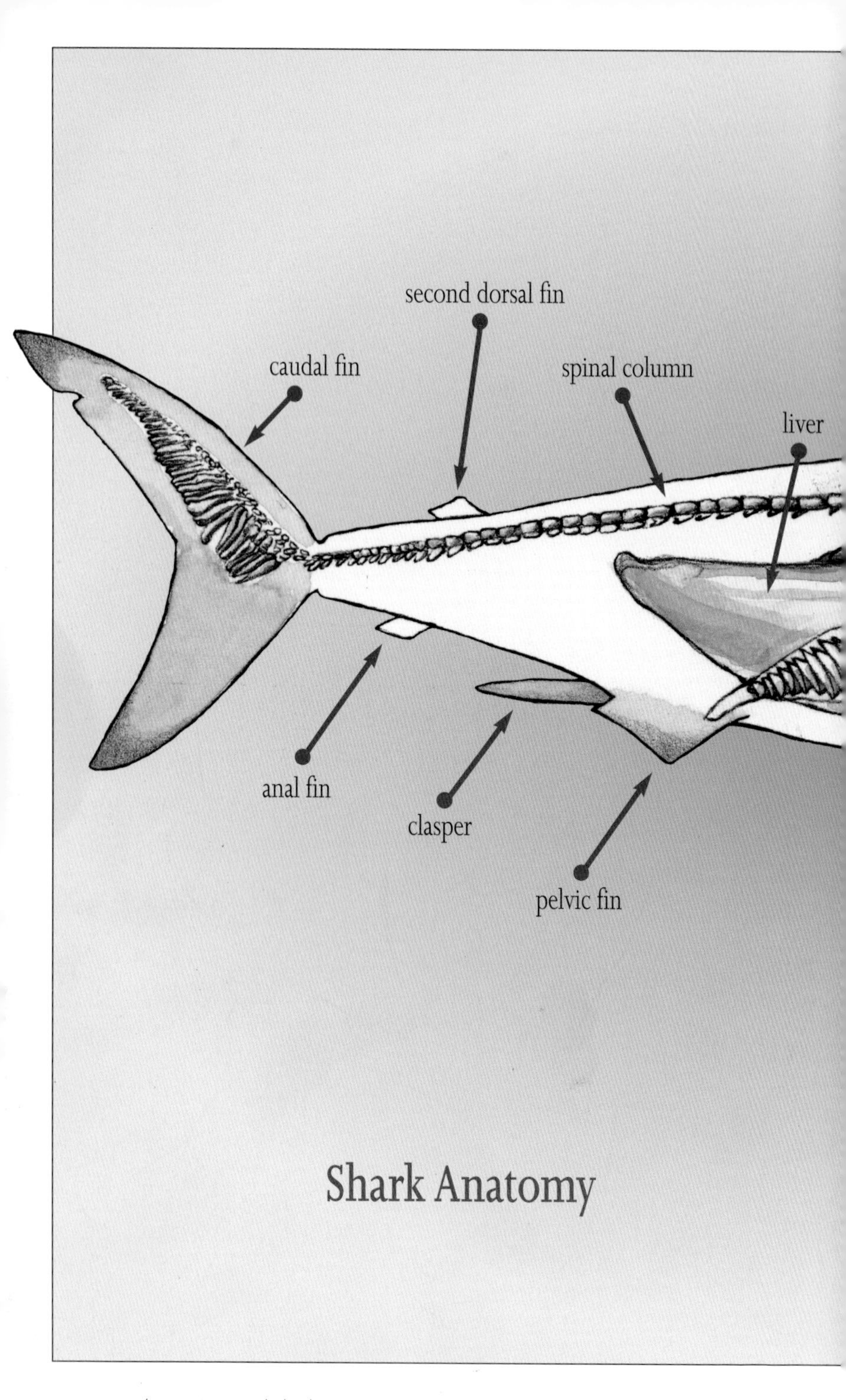

Shark Anatomy

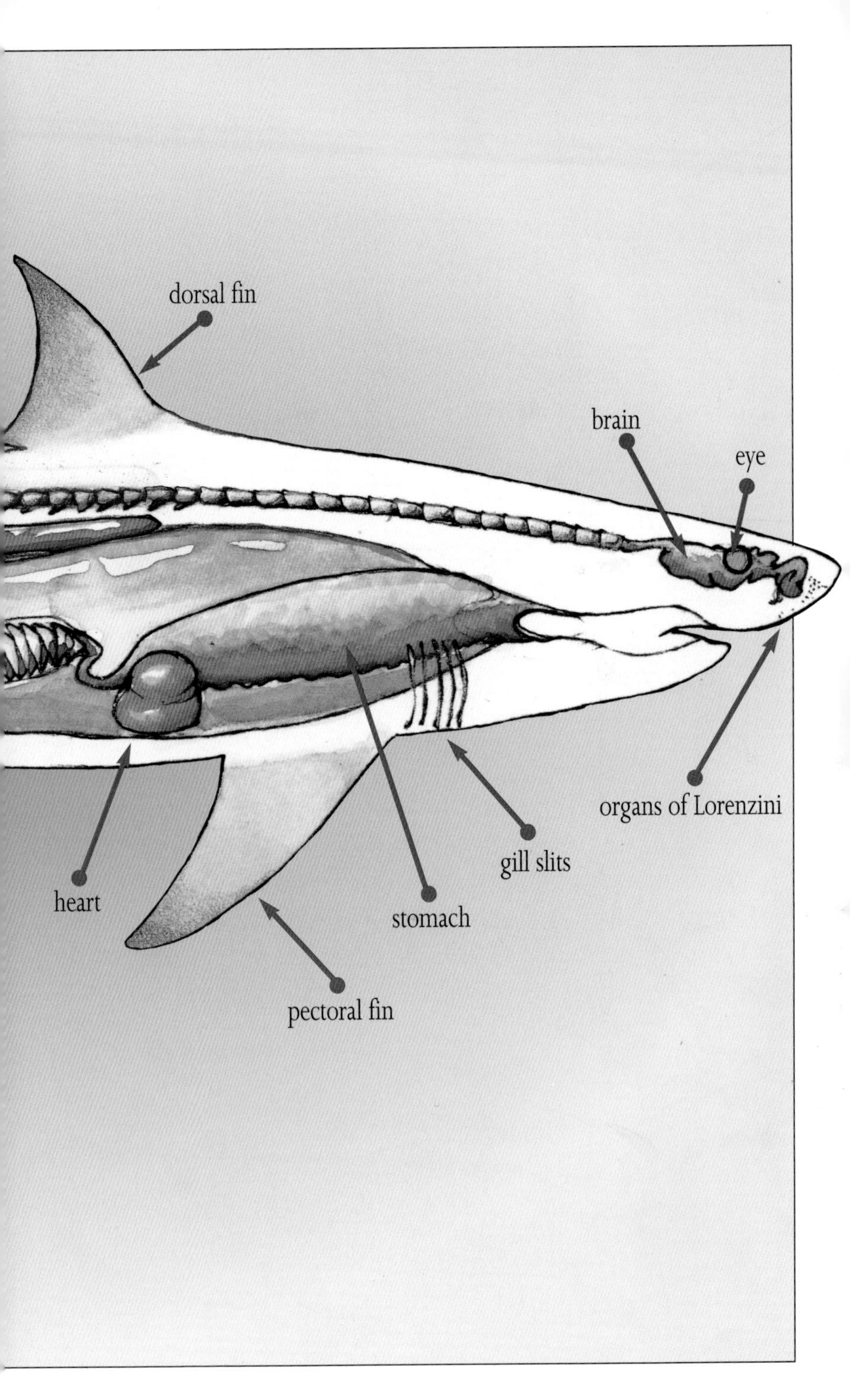
dorsal fin
brain
eye
organs of Lorenzini
gill slits
heart
stomach
pectoral fin

Unlike bony fishes, most sharks can't control their fins, except for the powerful side-to-side movement of their tails. One reason some sharks can swim quickly is that their vertebrae run all the way to the end of their tails. Not only does the tail move a shark forward, it also lets sharks change direction quickly. The other fins work to keep sharks stable in the water. The pectoral fins are like an airplane's wings. They keep the shark upright as long as it keeps moving forward.

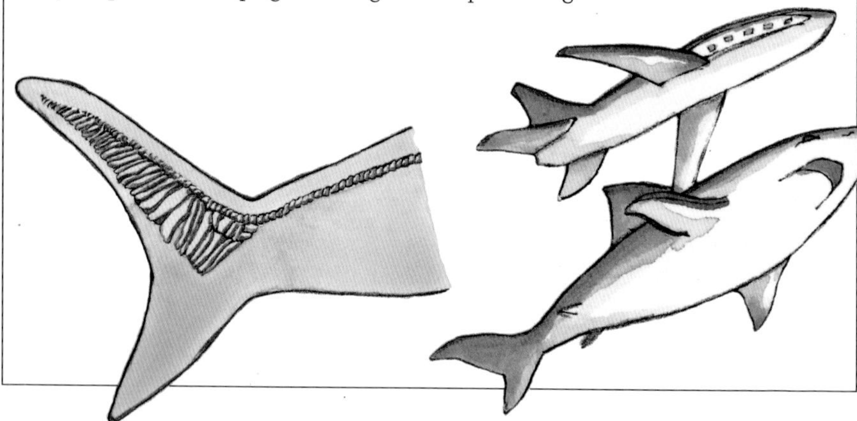

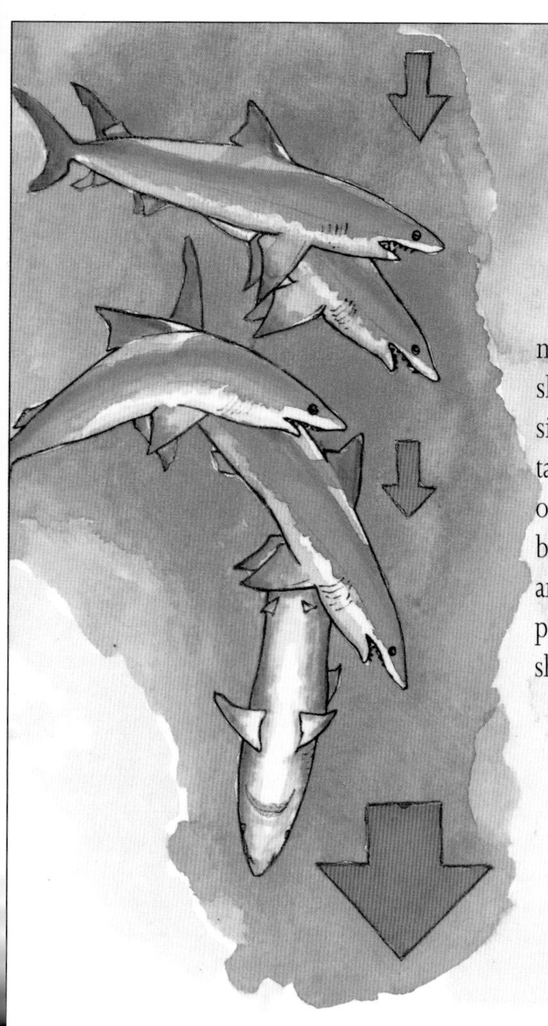

Most sharks have to keep moving forward and heading slightly upward or they will sink. This is especially important for sharks that swim in the open ocean. The bottom may be miles down, where it is cold and dark, and where the water pressure is too great for the sharks to survive.

Some sharks need to keep swimming in order to breathe, too. When they swim forward, water passes into their mouths and then out over their gills, allowing them to draw oxygen from it. When they stop moving, the water stops flowing, and they can suffocate.

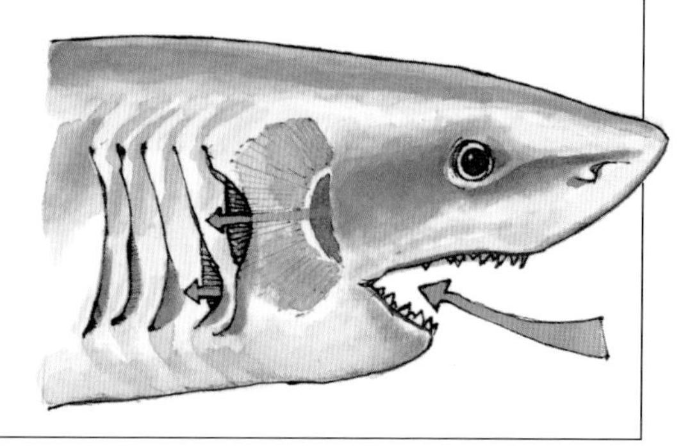

Most fish have something called a gas bladder, which they can fill with gas. Since gas is lighter than water, it keeps the fish from sinking.

But sharks don't have gas bladders. Not having them helps sharks move quickly from one depth to another because they don't have to constantly adjust their gas bladders.

Some sharks have huge, oily livers that keep them from sinking too fast. In some sharks the liver occupies as much as 90 percent of the body cavity and makes up 25 percent of the weight. The basking shark's liver can weigh 1,000 pounds! That sounds heavy, but the liver produces lighter-than-water oils that decrease the density of the shark's body and allows species like the basking shark and the whale shark to lie almost motionless at the water's surface. The less dense the shark, the less quickly it will sink.

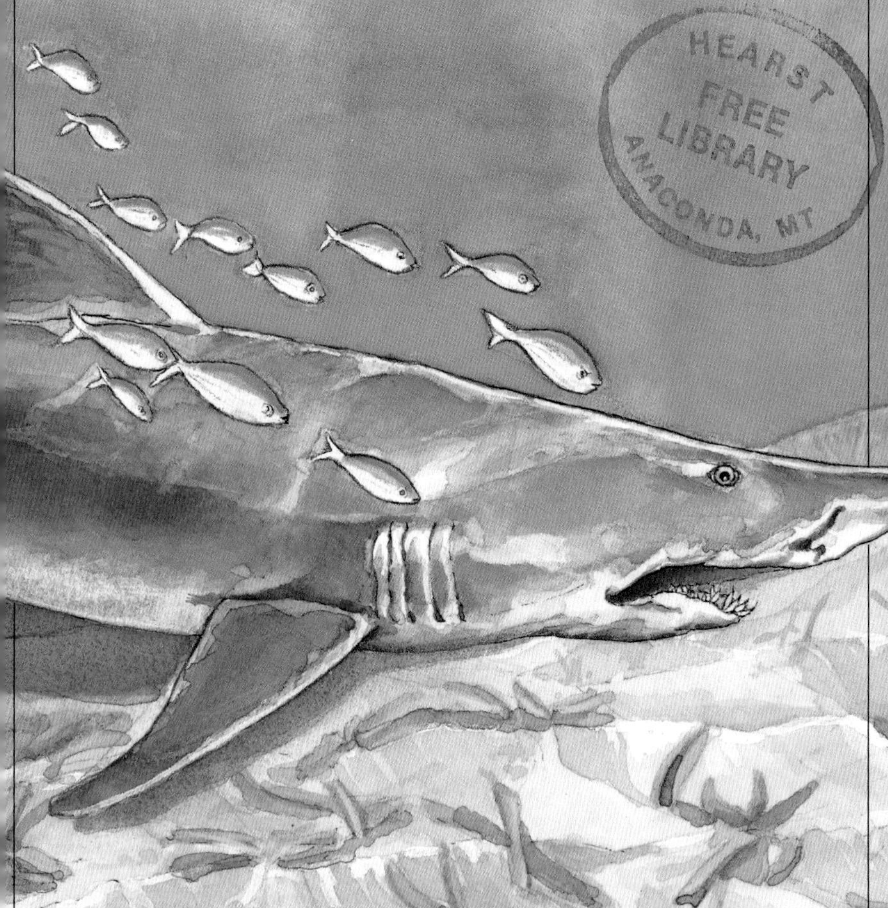

Sand tiger sharks spend a lot of time floating just above the ocean floor, where they rest and eat.

For them, sinking is a good thing, while for many sharks it would be a disaster. To keep themselves off the bottom, they swallow a gulp of air before they dive. Scientists have seen these sharks releasing air in "burps."

Bringing sharks together to mate can pose a problem. Some sharks are happy to eat members of their own species. Luckily, sharks seem to lose their appetites when it's time to mate. Females also lose their appetites when they give birth to their pups. Otherwise they might eat them, too.

Some sharks lay eggs. Different kinds of sharks have different kinds of egg cases.

Tendrils secure egg cases to coral, seaweed, or rocks where they are hidden from predators.

Other sharks give birth to live young. Newborn sharks are called pups. They emerge from their mothers fully formed and ready to fend for themselves. But they aren't exactly cuddly pets. In fact, sometimes, when a ragged-tooth shark is pregnant, the largest pup will eat its brothers and sisters before they are born.

Our parents only had two kids. How many do sharks have?

All depends on the species of shark.

Some sharks have a lot of small offspring. Nurse sharks have 20-30 pups: each one is about a foot long. Tiger sharks can have as many as 80 pups. In general, if a shark is born small it is more likely to be eaten by other sharks or large fish. Having more offspring increases the chance that some will survive. Others have only a few pups, but they can be very large. The great white has about six offspring, but they may be over four feet long when born. Very few predators could safely attack a newborn great white.

Most sharks are solitary animals. But the most common shark on the Pacific and Atlantic coasts of North America travels in large groups. They are called spiny dogfish and swim in "schools" that sometimes include thousands of individuals. These groups are usually broken into five smaller groups based on size and sex: Mature males swim in one group. Mature females swim in another. Young males and females each swim in their own groups. Small, immature sharks of both sexes swim together in their own group.

In America, fishermen who catch spiny dogfish sell them to be made into fish meal, which is mostly used for feeding chickens. In the United Kingdom, these sharks often are the fish in "fish and chips."

Remoras have suction cups on the tops of their heads, which allow them to stick to the undersides of sharks, even when the sharks are swimming very fast. The sharks like to have remoras around because they eat pesky little parasites, animals that live on the sharks' skin. When a shark catches prey, the remoras let go and help themselves to some of the scraps. So the sharks help the remoras and the remoras help the sharks. This kind of relationship is called symbiosis. But it is not a perfect friendship. Sometimes the shark eats the remora.

The remora's powerful sucking action has made it useful as a fish hook in Cuba and other parts of the world.

A fisherman ties a thin line around its tail. When he sees a big fish or a turtle, he tosses the remora into the water. The remora swims out and gets a good grip on the prey. Then the fisherman pulls the catch out of the water.

Pilot fish follow sharks around, staying very close to them but not actually hanging on. Like remoras, pilot fish eat the scraps when a shark catches prey. But unlike remoras, pilot fish don't actually help sharks in any way. Though they don't harm them either. This kind of relationship is called commensalism.

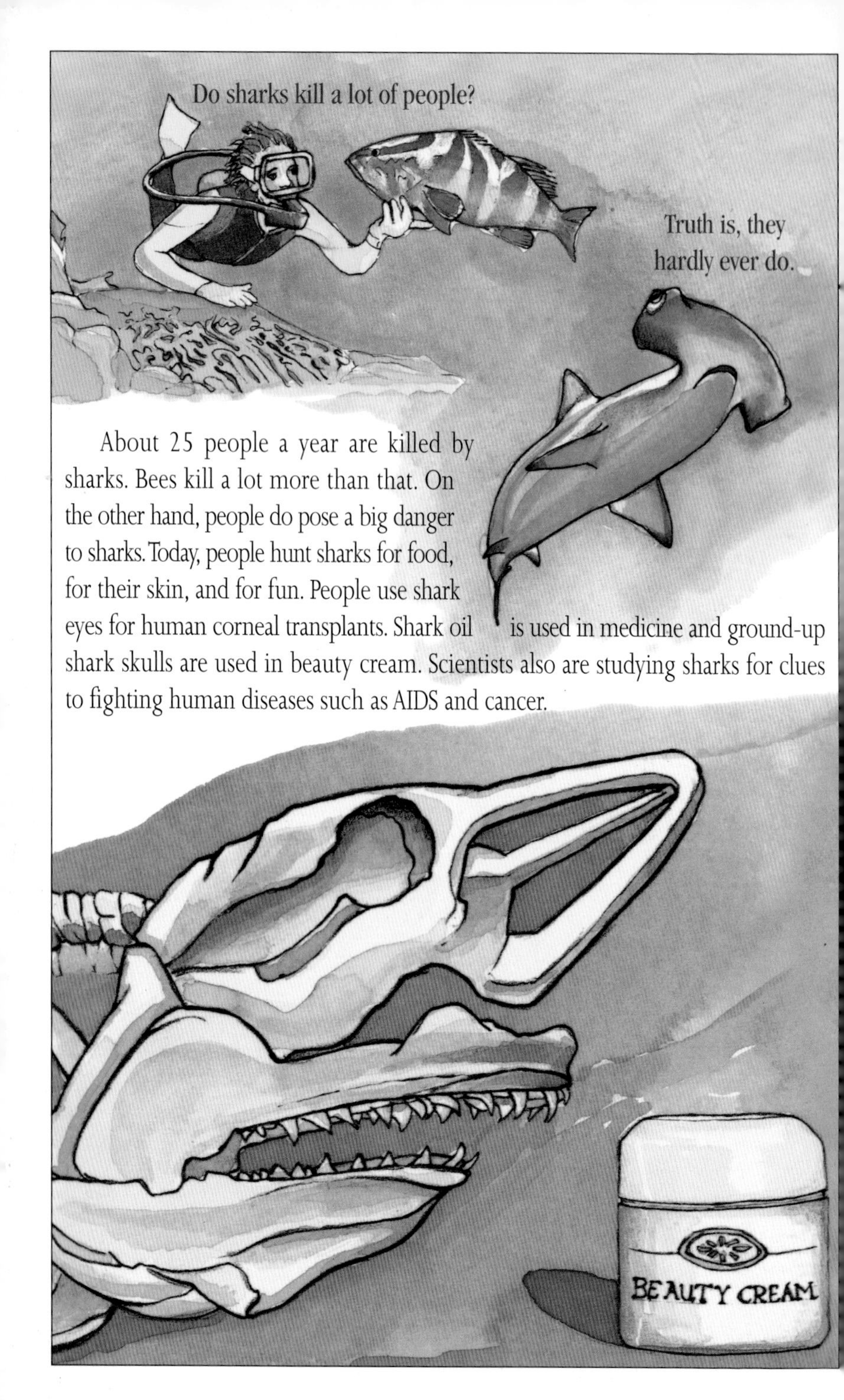

About 25 people a year are killed by sharks. Bees kill a lot more than that. On the other hand, people do pose a big danger to sharks. Today, people hunt sharks for food, for their skin, and for fun. People use shark eyes for human corneal transplants. Shark oil is used in medicine and ground-up shark skulls are used in beauty cream. Scientists also are studying sharks for clues to fighting human diseases such as AIDS and cancer.

People have probably always eaten sharks. The problem is that today people are killing too many. The U.S. Department of Commerce estimates that people kill more than 100 million sharks a year. Sharks take a long time to reach reproductive maturity and many species have relatively few offspring. So it is hard for shark populations to recover from overfishing by humans.

Some fishermen hunt sharks only for their fins, which some people like to eat in soup. When they catch a shark they cut off its fins and sometimes throw the shark back into the ocean. Without its fins a shark can't stay upright in the water. If these sharks don't bleed to death, they soon die of starvation or exhaustion.

Humans cause other problems for sharks, too.

Pollution harms sharks. And it's not just spilled oil and discarded garbage. There are so many people in the world today, and they use up so much energy, that they may be raising the temperature of the world's oceans. This could make life difficult for sharks that need particular habitat conditions. Of course, these aren't only problems for sharks. Pollution and climate change will affect all living things on Earth. Including people.

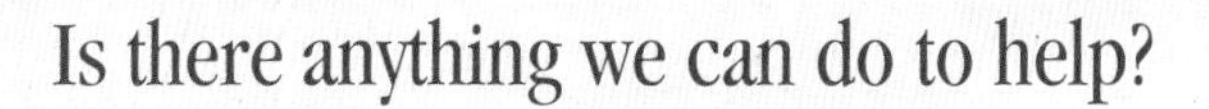

Is there anything we can do to help?

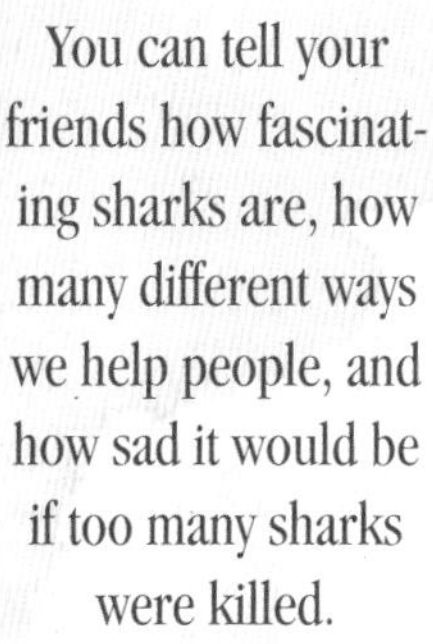

You can tell your friends how fascinating sharks are, how many different ways we help people, and how sad it would be if too many sharks were killed.

The better people get to know us, the more they will respect us.

I wonder what we'll do for *my* birthday?

So long for now.

Glossary

cartilage: strong, flexible tissue

chondrichthyes: cartilaginous fish including skates, rays, and sharks

classification: a systematic arrangement of groups of organisms that reflects its ancestry

commensalism: a relationship between two kinds of organisms in which one provides some benefit while the other neither provides benefit nor exacts harm

denticles: tooth-like structures on the skin of sharks

evolution: the process by which species change over generations

gas bladder: organ allowing most fish to float in water

gills: organs used by fish to extract oxygen from water

genus: taxonomic category including all the species of a particular type

offspring: descendants

organs of Lorenzini: organs, around the mouth of many sharks, that sense electrical impulses

parasite: a creature that lives on or in another creature often taking food or other benefit from it

pelagic: living in the open ocean

plankton: tiny organisms that live in water

predator: animal that lives by hunting and eating other animals

prey: animal hunted and eaten by other animals

siblings: offspring of the same female

species: animals of a particular type

symbiosis: two different species which live together, usually beneficial to both

tendrils: tissue used to attach shark egg cases to plants or other material